For Errolyn, Zoë (Zoya), and their families

—E.J.

For Mom and Dad, with love

—L.C.

www.fsgkidsbooks.com

Library of Congress Cataloging-in-Publication Data
Jenkins, Emily, date.
    What happens on Wednesdays / Emily Jenkins ; pictures by Lauren Castillo.— 1st ed.
        p. cm.
    Summary: A child describes every event that occurs on a Wednesday, from waking up
while it is still dark out and deciding it is not a kissing day, through a half-day of school,
to snuggling into bed at night.
    ISBN-13: 978-0-374-38303-9
    ISBN-10: 0-374-38303-0
    [1. Day—Fiction. 2. Parent and child—Fiction.] I. Castillo, Lauren, ill. II. Title.

PZ7.J4134 Wha 2007
[E]—dc22
                                                                                          2006040854

What Happens on Wednesdays

Emily Jenkins   Pictures by Lauren Castillo

Frances Foster Books • Farrar, Straus and Giroux • New York

What happens on Wednesdays is I wake up when it is still dark out.
Mommy comes in wearing her sleeper suit and swings me up and kisses me.
I tell her today is not a kissing day.

I sit on the counter while Mommy makes coffee.
Then she drinks her coffee and I drink my milk
and maybe we have some strawberries while we
read stories on the couch.

When the clock says six, we wake up Daddy.
Which can take a long time.

Daddy and I go down to get the newspaper.
I help him take off the rubber band.

Then he drinks tea in the flower chair and I sit on his lap. Mommy goes around straightening things and makes my lunch. I remind her to put in animal crackers.

When the sun comes up, I look out the
window for the shop across the street to open.
A cat steps out and smells the morning.
Her name is Maria.

Mommy says, "Bye, love. I'm going in the back
to work on the computer." She kisses Daddy
and tries to kiss me, but I remind her that
today is not a kissing day.

Daddy and I get dressed and we go out, past Maria and the shop where she lives, past my friend Errolyn's building,

past the daycare where I used to go when I was little, across the street, and down the block to the bagel store by the dog park.

"Two poppy seed, toasted, with cream cheese," says Daddy.
"And a large black coffee."
"Oui," says the man behind the counter, because he is French.

We buy an orange juice that comes with a special little straw and take
our food to the dog park so we can sit at the picnic tables.

My friend Zoya is there with her dad. She gets up early, too. I give her some of my bagel. Then Zoya and I run from tree to tree and go down the curly slide.

Soon, the dogs come into the park for their walks. Tiger and Trouble and Harlem and Peaches and Sanchez. Tiger and Peaches look the same as each other. Tiger goes off his leash.

When it is time, Daddy and I say bye to Zoya and walk past the store with the toy mouse you can ride for a quarter, and around the corner to school.

I put my coat in my cubby. What happens on Wednesdays is there are bubbles in the water table, so I play with that, and Daddy says goodbye. I remind him that today is not a kissing day.

We have choice time,
and circle,
and choice time,
and music,
and playground time,
and stories,
and lunch.

Which is the same on Wednesdays as any other day.
I eat my animal crackers first.

Mommy picks me up after lunch, and we go home and drink milk and read books in the big grownup bed until we both fall asleep.

What happens on Wednesdays is when I wake up from my nap, Mommy has her bathing suit on under her clothes and we go to the pool.

There's a lady in the locker room who says I'm delicious, and I like to get inside the lockers.

There are rubber ducks and foam noodles in the pool during Family Dip.
I always get a purple noodle. I can put my face in. I cry in the shower
because I don't like it. Then we dry off and put on our clothes and
Mommy gives me a granola bar from her pocket.

On the way home, we stop at the library, which has a stuffed duckling that's big enough to ride on. There are shelves of scary grownup stories that spin around if you push them. I sit on the counter while Mommy checks out books.

Then we go down the steps, up the block where we once saw an umbrella caught in a tree, past the bakery where we got that chocolate croissant,

across the street, past the daycare where I used to go when I was little,
past my friend Errolyn's building, past Maria and the shop where she lives,
to home.

Mommy makes my dinner. I put Band-Aids on Looga, my stuffed
elephant, or I make a puppet show, or I build a swimming pool out
of blocks, or I go through the laundry and try on grownup clothes.
It is different every Wednesday.

What happens on Wednesdays is Daddy comes home early. I eat my dinner and share some with him. Then Daddy gives me a bath. I can put my face in.

I put on my sleeper suit and do the zipper myself. Then Mommy reads stories while Daddy unloads the dishwasher. Or Daddy reads stories while Mommy goes around straightening things. And what happens on Wednesdays is I can pick who puts me to bed. So I pick Daddy.

I say good night to Mommy, and remind her today is not a kissing day.

Daddy and I go in my room, and Looga comes, too. We turn out the light. I remind Daddy that today is not a kissing day, and then I kiss him, and he kisses me, and I kiss him, and he kisses me.

He sits on my bed, quietly. I close my eyes, but then I open them again. I can see my hands in the dark. I can hear Daddy breathing. And that is all. That's what happens on Wednesdays.